The Name of the Child

To my late grandparents, Esther and Harry Boden,
brave pioneers and memorable storytellers.
MR

For Lauren and James
DK

The Name of the Child

written by Marilynn Reynolds and illustrated by Don Kilby

Orca Book Publishers

Lloyd was afraid of strange dogs and lightning. He was afraid of the dark, and he was afraid of getting lost.

"Don't make me go on the train by myself," he begged Mother.

"It's not safe for you to stay in the city," Mother told him. "Thousands of people are sick with influenza. You'll be safer at Auntie Alice and Uncle John's house in the country." She hugged him. "And you'll get to see their new baby!"

As the train steamed out of the station, Lloyd worried. What if Uncle John and Auntie Alice forgot he was coming? What if there was no one there to meet him?

Hours later, Lloyd stepped down from the train. There stood Uncle John.

"Auntie Alice is home with the new baby." Uncle John smiled. "He's only four days old. He's so new we haven't even chosen a name for him."

"And that is Old Bob." Old Bob turned his great head around to look at Lloyd. "He's awfully big," Lloyd said.

The wagon lurched and jolted over the rough roads. Hawks soared above them, dipping and diving in the late summer sunshine like kites on a string.

"Do bears or wolves live around here?" Lloyd asked.

Uncle John laughed. "Not many bears or wolves, but we do have lots of coyotes," he said.

Lloyd nestled closer to his uncle's side.

Uncle John looked down at him in surprise. "They won't hurt you," he said. "They're afraid of loud noises and they only eat rabbits and gophers. If you listen tonight you'll hear them howling."

Auntie Alice smiled at Lloyd. "I'm glad you're here," she said. "Now come and see our little son. We still haven't decided on a name."

The new baby was wrinkled and red, the smallest baby Lloyd had ever seen. When Lloyd held out a finger, the baby clutched it with his tiny hand. "He's strong!" Lloyd gasped.

"Would you like to hold him?" Auntie Alice asked, but Lloyd shook his head. "Maybe tomorrow," he said.

In bed that night, Lloyd tried to think of a name for the new baby, but nothing seemed to suit that little red face. He had just closed his eyes when he heard a voice, high and lonely. The voice was joined by other voices and they sang together. Coyotes. Coyotes hunting at night. Lloyd felt a stirring of fear, but the strange coyote voices faded as he fell asleep.

The house was quiet when Lloyd woke up the next morning. When he went out to the kitchen the woodstove was cold. Uncle John came out of the bedroom in his nightshirt. His face was pale. "Auntie Alice and I were sick all night," he said.

Uncle John sat down and laid his head on the kitchen table. "You'll find bread and plenty of food in the cupboard. I'll go out and feed Bob, then I'm going back to bed." He tried to smile. "We'll be better this afternoon," he promised.

Lloyd spent the whole morning alone. What if Auntie Alice and Uncle John had the flu? He wandered around the house. There was no radio or telephone. When he looked out the window there were no other houses in sight.

By afternoon, there was no sign of Uncle John or Auntie Alice. The baby's cries filled the house. Fear rose inside Lloyd.

To make himself feel better, he began to sing:

Rock-a-bye baby on the tree top,
When the wind blows the cradle will rock.
When the bough breaks the cradle will fall,
And down will come baby, cradle and all.

That last line was no good. Lloyd thought and thought. Then he sang the song again. This time it finished with a new line, "And Lloyd saves the baby, cradle and all."

That was better. So much better that Lloyd sang the song all afternoon. Over and over and over.

Evening came. The house turned dark and cold. Finally, Uncle John stumbled out of the bedroom with the baby in his arms. "Alice is terribly sick," he said. "And there's no milk for the baby."

Lloyd stared at him. "Do you think it's influenza?" he whispered.

Uncle John nodded. His forehead was covered with drops of sweat. "You and the baby have to get away from here," he said.

He came closer. Lloyd took a step back.

"Auntie Alice's friend, Mrs. Edwards, lives on a farm near here," Uncle John said hoarsely. "She has a telephone. She could call a doctor. And she has a milk cow. You must take the baby to Mrs. Edwards."

"But I don't know how to get there," Lloyd cried. "I don't know how to drive Old Bob   and it's almost dark!"

"The baby has to have milk," Uncle John replied. "Flu is catching. You must go to Mrs. Edwards. Just sit in the wagon with the baby on your lap. Old Bob will take you there."

Then Uncle John lowered his voice. "I can't leave Auntie Alice," he said.

Uncle John staggered out to the barn. He led Old Bob into the yard, but he was too sick and dizzy to hitch him to the wagon. With trembling fingers, Lloyd fastened the harness just as Uncle John told him. Old Bob seemed giant and dangerous. Lloyd kept well away from his hooves.

Lloyd climbed into the wagon, and Uncle John laid the baby in his arms. "Mrs. Edwards' house is only five miles west," he said. "Watch for the lamp in her window."

"But you said that Old Bob knows the way," Lloyd cried.

"Yes, yes, Old Bob knows the way. But watch for the light," Uncle John repeated.

"What if we get lost?" Lloyd exclaimed.

Uncle John knotted the reins and threw them over Lloyd's shoulder. "Gee up!" he mumbled. Old Bob pulled the wagon across the farmyard and out onto the road.

Lloyd's heart beat like a hammer as the wagon bumped and swayed. The baby was warm and heavy in his arms. When he heard a snuffling sound, he darted a glance down. The baby was holding his fist in his mouth and sucking it fiercely.

Lloyd felt a rush of pity. "We're going to get milk for you, little baby-with-no-name," he said. "I'll look after you." He held the baby closer.

The terrible sound of thunder made Lloyd start. The sky was black. Lightning flashed across the clouds, followed by more thunder. Then rain.

The rain poured from the sky, running down Lloyd's neck and onto the baby's blanket. Lloyd pulled his cap down around his ears and crouched forward to protect the baby.

The dirt road turned to mud. It was harder to pull the wagon now. Old Bob labored and heaved.

"Hurry!" Lloyd shouted to him. "It's almost night."

Hobbled by the mud, Old Bob moved more and more slowly. The wagon creaked along, inch by inch.

Lloyd was sure coyotes were watching from the bushes. An hour or more passed before he finally saw a light, tiny, far away and winking in the rain. His heart lifted. It must be Mrs. Edwards' farm.

Old Bob saw the light too. He veered to the left to pull the wagon up the narrow side road to the farmhouse, just as he'd done so many times before.

But as he made the turn, the wagon slid sideways in the mud. Old Bob struggled, but the wagon tilted off the road and stuck fast.

Lloyd clung to the baby as the wagon settled into the ditch. "Come on, Bob!" he shouted. "Gee up! Gee up!" he yelled.

The horse strained against the traces, but the wagon didn't move. "Gee up! Gee up!" Lloyd shouted again.

With a wheeze, Old Bob stopped pulling. He looked around the ditch for some grass and began to eat.

Lloyd trembled as he soothed the crying baby. "Shhh, shhh, little baby-with-no-name," he said. "Don't cry. I'll carry you. I'll look after you."

With shaking knees he climbed down from the wagon. He wrapped the blanket closer around the baby. Old Bob watched them as they started down the road.

Lloyd's boots stuck in the heavy mud. He stumbled. "It's all right. It's all right," he told the baby.

Just then he thought he saw something glittering in the bushes beside the road. Glittering like eyes. Was it a coyote? Hadn't Uncle John told him that coyotes were afraid of loud noises? I'll sing, he thought to himself. I'll sing!

Taking a deep breath, he sang his song as loudly and boldly as he could:

> *Rock-a-bye baby on the tree top,*
> *When the wind blows the cradle will rock.*
> *When the bough breaks the cradle will fall,*
> *And Lloyd saves the baby, cradle and all.*

Lloyd sang in the lightning and the thunder. He sang to stop the baby from crying. He sang to scare away the coyotes.

He sang to make believe he was brave.

Once he slipped and sat down in the muck, but he held the baby tightly and struggled back to his feet.

He trudged through the rain, still singing. He plodded on toward the light and into the farmyard. He pushed on through the mud to the front door of the house and banged with all his might.

It seemed forever before the door opened and an old woman stood in front of him.

"Phone the doctor, Mrs. Edwards!" Lloyd shouted through the rain. "Phone the doctor! Uncle John and Auntie Alice are sick. Very sick. With the flu! And the baby needs milk. And Old Bob's stuck in the mud with the wagon."

As he placed his small, hungry bundle into the woman's arms, Lloyd began to cry.

"I sang," he said through his tears. "I sang all the way."

One week later, Old Bob brought Lloyd, the baby and Mrs. Edwards back to Uncle John and Auntie Alice's house.

Auntie Alice held her baby for a long time. She kissed Lloyd. She hugged Mrs. Edwards. Then she looked down at the baby.

"We've thought of a name for our son," she said. "His second name will be Edward, for my good friend Mrs. Edwards who looked after him and who phoned the doctor." She smiled at Mrs. Edwards.

She looked at Lloyd with an even bigger smile. "And we've chosen a very special first name—the name of the brave boy who carried our baby through the mud and the rain. His first name," she said, "will be Lloyd."

First published by Orca Book Publishers

Orca Book Publishers gratefully acknowledges the support for its
publishing programs provided by the following agencies: the Government
of Canada through the Book Publishing Industry Development Program
and the Canada Council for the Arts, and the Province of
British Columbia through the BC Arts Council and the
Book Publishing Tax Credit.

Design by Christine Toller

School Edition
ISBN 0-13-205822-7
Distributed by
Pearson Education Canada
26 Prince Andrew Place
Don Mills, Ontario
M3C 2T8

Printed and bound in Canada
2 3 4 5   MP   10 09 08 07